Riding The Night Mare And Other Poems

by

Andrew L. Roberts

For Kazue…always.

And for those friends still here.

3

Also by Andrew L. Roberts

Feathers Wax and Dreams

Duramen Rose

Kite Shadows and Smaller Secrets

Table of Contents

My Eulogy

How

n the end

will you remember me

and with what words

good

husband

brother

author

friend

or as one-half of one of my

creations

some small portion

of the flesh and blood and bone

the words

the voice

the last honest breaths of one

Duramen Rose

I can think of worse ways

to be remembered

and not many better

and these I hope are the

most true

that I have been

a good husband

brother

author

friend

and

some portion

of the flesh and blood and bone

the words

the voice
the last honest breaths of
Duramen Rose.

Riding the Night Mare

Is it the calliope's piping
that sends these horses
rearing
wild eyed
manes flying
hooves beating
at the air
racing in place
but getting no further
as the carousel turns
and turns and turns

or is it the voices
of children
high on sugar
cotton candy
pink popcorn
and the hypnosis
of too many colors
and enchantment of
carnival and cowboy
dreams
of brass rings
Annie Oakleys
and the promises of
endless rides
and eternal summers

or is it fear
and the knowing

that there is no escape
from the unending agony
of being impaled by a pole
and bridled with an iron bit
forever jammed
between their teeth
silencing their cries
and pleas
for mercy
for freedom
and for release
seeing this
seeing them
I can never look
into their eyes
again
or bear to hear
that sound
of the calliope's piping
the carousel's engine
growling
the hungry shouts of
insatiable children
the cries of barkers
and the silence
of wooden horses
being tortured
for a child's pleasure.

As the Dead Man

As the dead man
in your deafened world
I will be silent now
carving my best words
into my own flesh
using the angel's feather
as a quill
and the dead language
of my father
and my mother
and of my time and place
I will turn away
cover my eyes with both hands
and walk in blindness
from this
your city and your century
so that my voice shall remain
my own
that I may sing myself
to sleep
and dream myself to
the place where I belong.

Fear

no one ever wants to admit
to being afraid
or of living their life in fear
day after day
no one wants to say
I am scared
worried yes - that's okay
but scared? no way
no one ever wants to admit
they are scared because
they are afraid
of being judged as
afraid
of being called a coward
afraid of being
a coward
but the truth is
I am afraid all the time
afraid of driving over bridges
afraid of high places
afraid of big crowds
and small spaces
afraid of Covid-19
and not being able to breathe
afraid of lung cancer
skin cancer
testicular cancer
heart attacks and diabetes
but mostly I am afraid
of failing
of losing my job

of failing my wife
of dying too soon and leaving her
alone
or of dying too late
and being left alone
of outliving everyone I love
it's true
nobody ever wants to admit
that they are afraid
and living every day of their life
in fear
but there it is
I have said it clear.

Goodnight

We say
goodnight
sometimes smiling
and finished with our
best sigh
but even for all of that
and anything else
what we truly mean
to say is
goodbye
because
underneath it all
is a whisper
and the knowing
that some night
and maybe soon
when we close
our eyes at last
everything might
disappear.

Unconditional

All dogs know a secret
shared among themselves
though likely learned from
cats
that human beings
by and large
are of two specific breeds
one being selfish and prone
to fits of cruelty
while the other
so kind
feeds them from their
own plate
speaks to them in their own
version of dog
— hoping for an answer —
while scratching in all
the right places
dogs know this
as do cats
and yet they treat both
types of men the same
because at the heart
of all things dog
is forgiveness
cats are somewhat more
pragmatic.

Tangerines

There are two
rather imperfect
tangerines
waiting
upon my desk
a pair of
rather imperfect
promises
left unspoken
to myself
sitting
within hand's reach
and even
without touching them
I know
how they will feel
I know the perfection
in the balance of
oil in their skin
and the way they will
fill this room
with their scent
as a natural perfume
when peeled
knowing so
makes my
mouth salivate
and sing
way back in the
tight corners of my
cheeks

it is important
essential even
to offer promises
to oneself
and keep them
within hand's
reach
especially
when they are
imperfect
but delicious
nonetheless
and so
now
there are two
rather imperfect
tangerines
waiting
upon my desk.

Atlas

You are
a gathering of maps
that defines not only you
but me as well
a snap shot of relationships
singular and communal
pulled together here
in one place and many
all at the same time
in spite of any artificial
time differences
our maps are more
geographical than political
expressed as mountains
and rivers
deserts
forests
farmlands,
cities
and islands
scattered in the midst
of our great seas
that roll in constant motion
each of us have our own
a place
that is natural to ourselves
but when puzzled together
we are almost borderless
with only small borders
fragile borders
thin and brittle borders

borders that more often

than not

are so blurred that each of us

each country

each state or province

is determined only by our

voices

our laughter

our tears

what we keep and

what we have lost or given

away

I do not always see

the shades of your skin

the colors of your eyes

your shapes or ages

or hear your accents

though when I am aware

of them

they are pleasing celebrations

of the size and splendor of

our shared world

boisterous

riotous

joyous

quiet even

and both a confusion

and revelation

mortal and divine

some people have no atlases

or maps

beyond those that are crammed

in a glove box
or forgotten in some
out of the way corner
of their unused library
but not mine
mine surrounds me even in my dreams
mine I carry with me everyday
wherever I might walk or rest
my atlas is alive
because
my atlas is all of you
we carry one another
upon our shoulders
and in our hearts
ceaselessly
under the same sky.

My Old Man's Eyes

When I think about my dad
I always see him from a distance
with lots of space between
us
sort of like Bambi only catching
glimpses of his father in the
shadows of the woods
or on a hilltop
from a stately distance
I hate to admit it
but when I think of my dad
the first and last images of his
face are the same
an unpleasant mask gone
unnaturally slack
and suddenly become a portrait
all in ash-grey and violet
with his green eyes closed
forever
I say green eyes but that's a lie
my dad's eyes were hazel colored
not really green
my eyes are green - truly green
but his were hazel
I'm pretty sure though that
I have his eyes at least in shape
I mean
that's how it looks in
the handful of photographs
I have of him
though I expect the emotions in

his hazel eyes
the laughter and the pain
were much stronger and deeper
than in my green eyes
I mean he was a father of five
and a soldier afterall
a marine
who fought in the second
world war
what do I know of real pain
or real laughter
not much by comparison
that's for sure
but still I think I have his eyes
and choose to believe it
and would likely throw a punch
if someone tried to say otherwise
I can still remember his voice
and I can really hear it if I try
we don't sound at all alike
though I've somehow picked up
some traces of his depression era
East Detroit pronunciations
I've only recently noticed this
after making friends with a couple
of women from Michigan
and that's a funny thing to hear
surrounded by all my
Northern California vowels
and Portuguese-American
consonants
but there it is

another bit of Dad
to go along with
my green eyes
sometimes
I try to imagine him dancing
I have been told
he was a fine dancer
which is funny and tragic
in that I can't dance a step
I don't have two left feet –
I have four
whereas my dad apparently
was quite a dancer
and I wonder how many
Michigan girls in his youth -
before he went to war
before he was wounded
before he came home
and before he met my mom
and married -
how many of those girls
fell for his laughing
hazel eyes
his big smile
and his excellent moves upon
the dance floor
I have no idea
and I am sure I will never know
he died you know when I was only
nine years old - and not even that
but at least I have his eyes
that's something isn't it

though the rest of me
is all from my mom side
the best parts probably that
have so far survived
but
if you really want to know about
my dad
you'll need to ask my older brothers
or our sister
they were here first
and are much older
and so would know
much better than I
about the old man
still though
we all have our dad's eyes
at least in shape
Joe's are brown
Rich's blue
Kevin's were brown too
but now closed
Mary's are hazel
and mine as I said before
are green
but I'll still say
mine are the closest to
and much the same
as the old man's who
died so damned young
and left me here to ponder
and fabricate maybe
all on my own

in the shadows of these woods
and at the base of this steep hill.

Red

I never cared much for
red
except for that bright
splash
on a blackbird's wing.

Spent

Forty-one years
honest work
a career
but less a
celebration now
upon reflection
than a sort of
protracted
exsanguination
of more
than just blood
but my youth
and my soul
my time
forty-one years.

Loyalty

They take your energy
first
and then they take your
soul
painlessly and in small
sips
more as vinegar than
wine
they buy your
enthusiasm
in forty hour lengths
tap
your youth
drinking both in gulps
until
your vision and your
hearing
start to go
innocence
follows next
along with the last of
your
youth and dreams
over time
and the passage
of decades
your hands loose their
strength
to grip
growing stiff and numb
and dead

then your heart goes
cold
and sours
and still you plough their
field
everyday
still
you break their stones
and hammer their
nails
everyday
turn
the wheel and the lathe
the lever and the crank
set pencil to ledger
filling
columns with facts and figures
because
it is the only thing you
know
or understand
it has become
who
and what you are
in your entirety
but
eventually
your vision
blurs
and everything fades
until
not even spectacles

can make a

difference

even with a lifetime of

experience

still your council is

ignored

because you are inconvenient

and

old

your loyalty has become your

liability

familiarity has bred

contempt

in those whose

wealth

you have helped create with

your

fool's sacrifice

and yet

saddest of all

you

only come to understand

the complete arc

of your own story

when it is too late

to change.

Evening

There is a taste
upon the air here
that accompanies
the chill
as evening slides
downward
towards the night
it is
a little bitter
sharp maybe
and familiar
though not so
much so as to
make me spit
I never noticed it
when I was young
but now
it's always
right there waiting
in all those black
feathered wings
turning and
gleaming
in the last bit of
light
that dies in a single
breath
at the very edge of
night.

Lost

I had discovered my audience
at last
in the old abandoned theater
an audience of dead men only
who wore their hunger
and their pain
in the sullen expressions of
their own defeat
they sat
silent and slumping back
within the tired wooden seats
covered in dust
and slowly being swallowed
by the stillness of the shadows
until
only the pale flame of the spirit lamp
burning upon the narrow stage
glowed within their empty eyes
and shined upon their teeth
watching and waiting
hungry
for me to reveal their stories
and give them back their
names.

Blind

How like that king of Thebes
I feel today
overwhelmed by the desire
to gouge out my own eyes
and walk away
for what I see is an ending
all in bitter slow motion
stealing ten thousand lifetimes
as slow as molten lead
punctuated by sudden calamities
that strike
as clockwork each day
after day
after day
I suppose the pantomime
of goodness
has lost its appeal in this nation
of entertainment and
the gun
what profits goodness
in hearts ruled by money
and the near-pornographic lust
for celebrity and attention
hope of any national salvation is
crumbling if not entirely gone
leaving only the forlorin hope
of those who might stand in the gap —
making one last suicide assault
against condemnation and the
boisterous and delusional howling
of counterfeit patriotism

cancelation and ridicule
with only the promise
of the eventual bullet
through the heart and through the head
as peace
where are such fools as these?
name them please
certainly not in any Senate
Capital or Statehouse
surely not among such men as these
for what prince
what king or councilor would dare
deny their constituents
the hot embrace of their
ArmaLite lovers
no
it is easier and safer
to make a speech
share a feigned grief
and lower one's eyes
call for prayer and let
ten or twenty children die
once or twice a week
and fifty two weeks each year
talk is cheap and votes expensive
and kings and princes and councilors
are cowards after all
fearing the assassin
as much as they fear the truth
and so I throw down these words
less a challenge and more a surrender
for in my heart I feel that this country

— this nation — I once knew and loved
has become the kingdom of the dead.

Indestructible

I miss the music
from before disco
and before compact discs
especially
all those bootlegged concerts
captured on cassette tapes
and 8 tracks
shared as secrets
The Moody Blues
Hawkwind
Pink Floyd
Yes
and The Blue Oyster Cult
big ballads
deep lyrics
solos
hunger and thirst
my only compass
riding with friends in their
Fords and Chevy's
late at night
riding shotgun
or lying across the backseat
feet up
windows down
seat belts sans shoulder harnesses
or no seat belts at all
just the promise
of one head trauma
or another
and all the laughter

God! the laughter
I miss your laughter
most.

Marathon 20-23

We raced
against death
with each other
and against each other
from March
and back again
to March
on through April
and into May
and still we raced
sometimes
stumbling
sometimes falling
barely able to get up
every movement
a reason to give up
until we could only
walk
upon shuffling feet
around the sun
from one more Spring
towards one more Summer
with that shadow still
at our heels and
at our lips
eager to steal
our last breaths.

No More

And so the seer speaks at last
upon the steps of the great house
saying
Rhamnusia knows your name
she has written it in backwards letters
with the venom your own words
upon the palm of her left hand
she will press it to your forehead
and leave it printed upon your flesh
then those who rejoice in your
sin of hubris
and celebrate in the shadows of your lies
and conceits
will see that Nemesis herself
has come
and come for them as much as you
the nation you have cracked in two
will shake itself to pieces
the wind
will blow through every open gate
every window
every door and every house
until your name is dust
and all the dust
is swept away
and your name is no more.

Easter Morning

This broken man
asks the question
heart and mind
aching
longing for an answer
pierced clean through
desperation
sunk deep within
flesh and bones
all the way down
to the marrow even
hands once only fists
open in surrender
a declaration
that the better man
has died for his
offences
understanding
that he may never know
the answer to his question
beyond hope alone
and the proud man
in return
asks the question too
a grin only
and a mockery
searching nothing
a punch line only
elevating himself
by stepping upon
the neck of

the broken man
who
prostrates himself
before God
making confession
asking for mercy
and the strength
to forgive the man
who stands upon
his neck
as he too was forgiven
for standing upon the neck
of another broken man
and the nails he has
hammered
daily.

Dumb

Some days
I just want to
shut up and
hear a different voice
in my head
saying something
innocent and shy
about freckles and
awkward first kisses
you know
that handful
of stumbling
stuttering
words
the words
that we only get to say
once or twice
with all the feelings
right up front
you know
before we all became
knowing and wise
and so damned
dumb.

Water

it is with the utmost clarity
that I recall
the first time I drank directly
from a stream
kneeling upon that tumble of
grey granite stones
reaching in with one cupped hand
lifting the water
so cold to my lips
so icy cold
making my teeth
feel as though
they would shatter like glass
and the taste
so fresh and pure and unlike
any other water
I have drunk since that day
left me refreshed
connected to the stream
and as alive
as the deer who watched me
from the other bank.

By Candlelight

The shadows were slippery

black snakes

hairy spiders

leftover nightmares

rippling over my knees

and

shimmying up the walls

a distraction from the guns

as I wrote the letter home

for my friend Tommy

who had lost most of his

words

and most of his

voice

leaving only the expression

in his eyes

to speak for him

that and my own understanding

which was pretty much worthless

the candlelight was oily

the wick sputtered and spit

but

the bombardment continued

it was a weak assault

punitive

impudent

impotent

rolling in at sunset

thunder without rain

but the pitiful thunder

of a blacksmith's hammer

pounding only
chalk and clay
not his anvil
so I ignored it
mostly
as I scribbled out the
words
I hoped would make some
sort of sense
for Tommy's sake...

Fiesta (a fragment)

It was Saturday
and the summer fiesta
near the small town of Madera
accordions pumping
trumpets and guitars
fanning the heat higher
and hotter
making us sweat
but in a good way
not bad
as the quiet men
with whom I worked
all weeklong
stacking lumber
and loading freight
cast off their silence
and their stern faces
and instead
sang their Mexican love
songs
to their sweethearts
and to their wives
who with their daughters
danced
weaving and turning in full circles
and figure eights
within one of the company's
double wide corals
they were butterflies at night
and not a moth among them
brilliant in their black skirts

with all those red and yellow
ribbons
all those roses and garlands
tied in their hair
singing their answers
to their men
promises and jests
made under the stars
and the crisscrossing
strings multi-colored lights
green and blue
yellow and orange
one girl with black curls
held me
with her eyes
and with her hands
pleading
bailor conmigo
in Spanish
and English
dance with me
dance with me Duryman
but I shook my head
no mas no mas
I said
and she feigned a sour face
then laughed
and danced off
by herself
to find a better man
with whom to
enjoy the music

cut loose
I threaded my way
through
the crowd and clamor
found the beer wagon
and an empty hay bail
and an unbroken view
of the stars
and there I tried to lose
myself for a minute or two
until I hear her say my name
again
Duryman
Duryman Rose.

The Newness of This Thing

Shiny
and fresh
alive
the way nothing else
has ever been
alive
glistening with dew
still sweet
crystal beads
of early morning light
captured
all blue-silver
red-fire and yellow-gold
wet
and new
so that I am transfixed
pierced clean through
by the very newness
of this thing
this fragile and unexpected
thing
that has been given
to me
this touch of spring
a gift from you
to me
while I was lost
and looking backwards
through the bare trees
of my sudden winter
given with a touch of

your hand upon mine
and your voice
soft and clear
a whisper like no other
that finds me whenever
I have grow weary
To lead me home again
to you.

War Surplus

See the soldier
on the street
his face a puzzle of
deep shadows
pale bones
some teeth remaining
and eyes hollowed out
by old sorrows
a bewildered somnambulist
hungry always hungry
homeless
now
walking in circles
a clock worn down
and run down
but refreshed by
the dreams he dreams
each night
and so
each morning
he is
reborn by those same
nightmares
a little less of himself
each day
see him clearly
the lines upon his forehead
the scars
the beet colored veins
that crawl over
his hands in gnarled vines

like sycamore leaves
in autumn
his long lean body
still tall but shrinking
thin in the failing light
a frame now only
for his war coat
he is a scarecrow
who no longer scares crows
but haunts himself
day after day
see him
the boy you sent away from
home
and robbed of
innocence and joy
all to fight the wars
you would not fight yourself
wars for profit and pride
see him now for who he is
see the mirror
see it clearly
see the face that you have
made
own it as your own
and do not look away
be haunted.

A View From The Grassy Knoll

I guess

this is what it must be like

sleeping

on that grassy knoll

softly snoozing

in all that yellow sunlight

comfortable and warm

oblivious

to the honey bees and butterflies

the buzzing and the kisses

and to the shouting — the shrieking

and the gunshots ticking away all

those innocent lives

as this dull parade of indifference

rolls on

and on

and on...

Hinnom

One good man struggles
among so many
climbs the sun-scorched hill
blood in his eyes and under
his nails
climbing with his hands and
with his feet
clawing at the yellow clay
and broken stones
his dusty cheeks
streaked by sweat and tears
he is becoming
less man than meat
but still he struggles
still he pleads
until he finds summit
and falls to his knees

It is only a low hill
and yet it affords some view
of his world
and what it has become
the open plain that was once
a valley
a plain of shattered and collapsed
sepulchers upon which
the lost mill and wander
shoulders bent under the
invisible weight of grief and
guilt and the weariness

of prolonged rage
it is a place of pain and ashes
without water or hope
though it was once called
home

The good man calls to those
below
reaches out for them
but none look up
the noon day sun is too bright
and so they fix their eyes
upon their own feet
following the ruts in the dust
that those before them have
left plowed with their passage
they follow now as they always
have
by habit
but they have lost their last leader
and their master now is the rut
itself
and the rut has no plan for them
no direction

The air sizzles
with the angry beating of wings
grasshoppers and larger locusts
swarm
raging in an insatiable hunger
that rides the wind and is
a madness to the ears

it cannot be silenced
louder than a thousand horns
it drones
it storms
proclaiming the names of
the damned
drowning out their last prayers
promising nothing
just the ceaseless droning
reminding them of who they
used to be
and the future they surrendered
to satisfy their hate and greed

And so
the good man weeps
and prays
until he is left with only
two words
to repeat again and again
Topheth
and
Hinnom
Topheth
and
Hinnom.

Writing

Writing
often requires walking
sometimes
without socks
in the dead man's shoes
through fire
and upon water
alone
and with only
your own words
for company
even
in a crowded train.

Comfort

This morning
I woke up to
the voice of
an angel
whispering
into my ear
saying
as underachievers
go
you've done
pretty good.

For Neil Mcintosh

turn off the noise
friend
turn off the lights
grab the coat
and find the leash
it's hanging by
the door
take the dog
for a walk
sing to the dog
your favorite song
and his
it doesn't matter
that it's raining
it's always raining
on days and nights
like these
what matters is
the dog
the song
the time you share
walking together
and this quiet cure
for the noise.

For the Jurors

So
here it is
go ahead and
tell me
my line breaks
could use some
work
tell me
my spacing
too
could use some
work
say
what you think you know
but
when my crow hops
upon a single
foot
circles
right before your
eyes
wings wide open
dancing
and cawing
telling you its greatest
secret
and mine
I know
you
will
not

hear
because
your only concerns
are with line breaks
and spacing
and what
you think you already know
leaving you
deaf
to my music
and blind
to my perfect
crow
dancing alone
before your window
all in a shimmer
of black feathers
and black silk
shining
in the morning light
wearing
a necklace
of dew.

For the Mudlarks

The river is a cemetery
where the Mudlarks gather
combing the banks for shiny objects
covetous crows
sifting the sand, the sludge, the pebbles
searching — always searching
greedy for bits of metal
charms, coins, roman rings,
and wedding bands
delighting in their finds
oblivious to the ghosts
who squat beside them
pining and remembering
how all those pretty things
once felt
when they held them in life
carried them in their pockets
and wore them upon their hands
but now their fingers are but
shadows
their bones long lost
to the current and to time
the Thames takes
after all
and the Thames gives
but the ghosts remain
and their curses linger
even now
upon all those shiny objects.

Savage and Entirely True

As a child
I saw my friends
everyday
inside and out
and they saw me
everyday
inside and out
we played together
on our lawns and
in the streets
we threw
homemade spears
peach pits
rocks
and our hardest punches
we gave each other
rope burns
Charlie-horses
bloody noses
and all of our deepest secrets
we loved without ever once
having to say the word
what we shared went
all the way to the bone
to the marrow
and into our blood
we were friends
and there was nothing tender
or delicate about it
frequently bruised
but never broken

it was tough as cobs
joyous
savage and entirely
true
making us somehow
immortal
as a child
I saw my friends everyday
and
as a man I seem them still
whenever I look inward
weighing the best parts
myself and
of who I have become
testing the weight of my
heart
against the weight of a
feather
I carry their names
all of them
in my flesh
in my scars
In my blood and in my bones
but mostly
in my heart
just as they still carry mine
in all the same places
all still whole
all true
and
immortal.

Oh Three One

You are
sleep
the mother of
dreams
sleep
the father of
nightmares
sleep
the teacher of
infinite possibilities
and sleep
the place where
first and last we
met.

Sleep

I am
wrapped
in an immortal coil
protected and embraced
enfolded and invulnerable
a witness to eternity
a part of the
universe itself
matter and gravity
the pull of light
overcoming
the dark
moment
by.

Musery

Come now
I seek the company of
tongue-tied dreamers
whose daily struggle
with rigid grammar
and its abandonment
leads to a song
where truth is wrung
coaxed or spun anew
from the inconsequential
and mundane moments
of life where magic hides
in plain sight.

Moment

You
gave me life
you give me
reason
each night
and each morning
newly born
my hope
my purpose
the very need
that keeps
my heart beating
the joy
and the yearning
of seeing a single
crow
in a cloudless sky
smelling red clover
and oranges
the fruit
and the blossom
touching silk
tasting your lips
hearing your sighs
and the bow

that draws a thousand
sighs
from the strings
of the most humble
instrument

sleep.

Slipping Into The Night

I remember that last afternoon
so clearly
it was a Saturday I think
though I am not certain
because all the days and nights
of that last week
had blended together almost
seamlessly
it was still daytime
I remember that
daytime sliding towards
the evening
February and winter
Valentines Day had just passed
and I remember the light
still bright but low
under the slow curtain
of clouds passing
beyond the big windowpane
wet from the earlier spattering
of rain
that had rattled briefly
as the rolling of a child's drum
a quiet though insistent tapping
it came suddenly
and then it left and was gone
I held your hand
watching you slowly receding
watching the pulse weakening
listening to your broken breathing
and knowing

it would not be long
you were winding down mom
and Mary
was upon the other side of the bed
holding your other hand
talking to you quietly
comforting you with nervous plans
of things that you would together
but she knew as well as I
that we had reached your final day
and were only waiting to say
goodbye
though
we did not want to say
goodbye
I faintly felt you squeeze my hand
tenderly
and saw you move you thumb
in such an intentional pattern
upon mine
and not much longer after that
you were gone
we called for your nurse
Hermi
with her stethoscope
she listened for your heart
then leaned in close
and said to you
rest in peace Bernice
and then at last
I cried.

Light

Ever since I was a child
I have sought illumination
more than simple knowledge
but the understanding
and greater still
some comprehension which
I would willing embrace
and so I live
imagining some great lamp
of beaten gold and bronze
and silver
shining
upon the unattainable horizon
ever out of reach
blazing brightly throughout
each day from dawn till dusk
coloring the sky with the pallet
of all creation
fire and water and your breath
cooling only with the night
allowing a time of respite from
that which drives me
even still though
the darkness is not whole
the stars offer a different kind of
illumination
softer and gentler
more encouraging than commanding
suggesting a course to the north
and bending my eye towards Polaris
soothing and cooling my daily fever

placing me in a small wooden boat
with two sad eyes painted upon its prow
and a triangular sail of glowing
parchment
but it is the moon I love most
changing shape throughout its cycle
yet always silver and sometimes
touched with lavender or blue when
the snow falls
and all of this light together
forms a coil within my heart
upon which my own words
are being written
and if I am quiet and still
and do not surrender
I will hear the light itself speaking
I will attain my goal
the illumination
which is your voice
alone.

You

You are the familiarity
of summer's sudden
sunlight
breaking through
a thousand shivering
green leaves
piercing my eyes and going
straight
to that place where all my
memories
are written with the letters
of your name
to form the perfect shape
of your lips
when we first kissed.

Death

There were a thousand
skipped heartbeats
caught and sewn
into those grey shadows
that clung so closely
to that woman's heels
following each footstep
of her rainy-day walk
meandering among
the shattered masonry
and bleached bones
of this dead city
so sorrowful
in her silence.

Guardian

My wife has a guardian angel
In the shape of a crow
a sweet beautiful bird
all onyx black and glossy
who comes to drink
from the fresh water bowl
she puts out every day
for Robbie
the neighborhood cat
but more often than not
it is this crow
who drinks from the bowl
and soaks its peanuts there
perches on our porch
and on our black mailbox
it likes to hang out with Kazué
as she works in our front yard
and back
following her upon the
red brick path
walking — not hopping
even calling to her at the window
when the water bowl is empty
this crow is so well behaved
it poops only on our neighbor's truck
but never on our car
and all in all I think this bird is

very cool and very fine
and I love that my wife is
watched over everyday
like Elijah
by her own guardian crow.

Ne'er Day

It is a narrow village
of narrow houses and narrow lanes
a town of
narrow thoughts and frugal hopes
diminishing
hugging close
the weathered cliff
its crooked backbone
that separates this old place
from the rest of the world
that has long since
pressed forward and moved on
seeking out a broader sky
in which to dream much wider
dreams

And yet
this is home
stubborn and defiant
back against that wall
forever facing outward
toward its storm-blackened sea
just as
mourners must face the open grave
stoically
with grief denied and bent inward
for none to witness or betray

Lichen-mottled, stone walls
lift seaweed-thatched rooftops

chimneys yet steam
with the last fires of
Hogmanay
but all the windows
are closed and shuttered fast
hands clapped over the eyes
protecting those ancient and
irreplaceable panes of glass
that the ancestors
brought to this island
when they first came
from the mainland far away

A cock crows
and soon another
as morning breaks
announcing
the first hour of daylight
though with daylight also denied
on this stormy new year's day
the wind and rain
have rendered everything
the same shade of wearied gray
that drowns the soul
and quenches any remaining
thirst to dream

And yet those dreamers
still awake
who stumble home
from their last merriments
of the now dead year

stagger with heads hanging
loosely from their shoulders
elbows, knees, and hips
near unhinged
the joints being too well lubricated
by too much whisky and dancing
some weep for nostalgia
some laugh for the same
and some so sick with their joy
and their regrets
that it is only by a miracle
that they will find their direction
home this day

Three such men
walk shoulder to shoulder
would-be-boxers
swaying and weaving
and still singing
they nearly collide with
the young, dark-haired stranger
coming down from the
port beyond the hill
seeing him
in the last moment only
they splinter
come apart
and roll
then when once he's past
come back together
and reassemble
arms again interlacing

over each other's shoulders
becoming a gate of three pickets
with one shared cross member
a crooked gate set free
windblown
rogue
and tumbling down the road
one man swears
another quotes Burns
and the third vomits
all over his companions
they curse together
until they laugh together
and carry on

But the stranger
strides onward
head down against the wind
with his singular purpose
undeterred
until he reaches his
destination
and knocks three times
upon the oak
of Sissy McKenzie's door

He gazes up at the house
before him
struck by what has changed
and struck deeper still
by what has remained unchanged
left bewildered by the truth

eighteen years have past for him
while eighty-seven
have passed for her
and though he has long known
this brutal equation
seeing the thing up close
is different than knowing it
as numbers upon paper
and of course
now there is no going backwards

Sissy
he says
trying to stand taller upon her step
a knapsack slung under one arm
and his Highland Pipes
wrapped in the old seal skin
tucked in close beneath the other
won't you rise
he says
and let me in
for I am the dark-haired man
for whom you've long hoped
I know you're weary
from waiting
and that your bones must
ache in this weather
but it is a new year
and I've returned
bringing gifts and a blessing
to your door
a bag of salt and a black bun

to grace your table
and sweeten your morning
whisky too
and a good dod of coal
for comfort and for warmth
and stories Sissy
— such stories and songs —
that you have never heard before
from distant stars and wider worlds
faraway
across the sky
beyond the blue and black

So
for Auld Lang Syne
listen to my voice
hear it and remember
it your big brother
Neil
who waits upon your step
come
open the door
and let me be the first foot
to cross your threshold
on this long overdue
Ne'er Day

In reply
there is a stirring
the rumor of footsteps
and floorboards
creaking

and the slipping of the chain
and bolt
that locks the door
the knob turns
and the door opens

Peering out is an old man
of seventy years or more
once fine features now
a roadmap of wrinkles
and a head balding
yet with some silver wisps
remaining
their eyes meet
and while there is recognition
in the old man's expression
Neil knows
they have never met
before
removing his rain-soaked
bonnet
and pushing back his hair
he repeats his name
but the old man only
nods
and motions for him to enter
saying
uncle, you are late
and this dark haired young man
replies saying
not too-late I hope
his fingers touching

the door's bolt and chain
his eyes questioning

Mother
says the old man
has me bolt the door
each Hogmanay
from midnight on
until midday
lest some other
enter by mischance
before you
stealing your
Ne'er Day

He motions again
for Neil to follow
and leads him to the room
where Sissy McKenzie
has been waiting
wrapped in a worn blanket
of storied tartan
propped up in her narrow bed
by three big pillows
and her small ragdoll
which has lost both its button eyes
and its red-stitched smile
to time

And Neil
sees now still more evidence

of time lost and misspent
for his sister has sorely been
diminished
reduced once more to the size
of the child she once was
tiny
but frail
and as ancient as the moon
and seeing this
the dark haired young man
of thirty-six summers
falls to his knees beside
his baby sister's bed
takes her hands between his own
enfolding them
with all the tenderness
he has carried with him
across the stars
from Farhaven in Orion's Belt
and Killthunder Station
where he lost his name to war
and New Alba on Finalshore
where he found it again
in peace

Sissy
he starts to say
but she stops his words
placing her fingertips
upon his lips
before letting her hands caress
and explore his impossibly

unchanged face

And
though Neil weeps
Sissy smiles
calls him by his nickname
chiding him for being late
again
and having no better sense
than to walk in the darkness
and the rain

And Neil
wanting to smile
but unable
hangs his head
and recalls the number
of all those harried jumps
between systems
when they skipped their ships
like stones
across the event horizons
of lightless singularities
slinging themselves
through the emptiness
between the stars
courting time
distorting time
cheating time
and forever losing the time
that passed too quickly
upon this island

in the unrecoverable decades
of a lifetime missed
that can never be restored

But Sissy
pinches his chin
until he meets her eyes
again
Whit's fur ye'll no go by ye!
she says
quoting their grandmother
stop your crying
she adds
I've lived long and I have lived well
sure I have missed you
but I am not yet dead
and though much is gone
 that could have been shared
some yet remains
I have only joy this morning
because
you are here
Neil
my only brother
returned from the dark
a blessing come home
flesh and bone
from across the stars
first footing my threshold
on this Ne'er Day

And Neil

nods and wipes his tears
away
reaches for his pipes that rest
beside his knee
should I play these now?
he asks
wake the neighbors as I used to?
or is it singing
that your heart desires
Auld Lang Syne perhaps
or the old Boat Song
that was your favorite?

But Sissy
shakes her head
No
she says
nothing old or familiar
play me
something shiny and new
something that will make me
feel as young as you
play me one of your own songs
brother
that you've brought home with you
from New Alba on Finalshore
let me see
those stars through your eyes
and all the places
where you've travelled
show me your life
all the way

from when you left this house
to your arrival
upon my doorstep
on this
my final Ne'er Day

Aye
says Neil
I can do that and more
and rising
he unwraps his pipes
and makes his way
back through the house
out the door again
down the narrow step
and back
into the gray dawn

Everything now
is still
the wind
has blown itself out
and the rain
that had harassed his steps
all through the night
is altogether gone
yet still the reluctant sun
plays the miser
refusing to show itself
and so Neil fills the bag
with his breath
bringing it to life

under his arm
his nephew joins him outside
unlatching the house's shutters
and throwing them wide
so that Neil sees his sister
inside
watching him from within
childlike in her expectation
her face beaming and angelic
in the firelight

With a sharp thrust
of his elbow
now
Neil strikes the drones
and begins the cèol mòr
that maps his life
starting as a slow air
sorrowfully climbing each note
one upon another
footsteps
unembellished
building the theme
of a seventeen-year-old
lad
neither eager for adventure
nor heroic in any way
just a lad
of easy laughter
with a love of his home
stifled by an uninvited duty
a lad

and no more than that
wishing to remain
with his mother and his sister
yet being marched away
from his father's funeral
leaving childhood behind
unfinished
shouldering a soldier's kit
and the family burden
assuming his father's debts
with a fifteen year enlistment
that has him marching off to war

This slow air continues
showing little haste
yet all the while
growing darker
and more determined
gathering in tempo
and in force
becoming a stormy theme
of thunder and the gale
adopting warlike courses
that echo the anthems of
The Black Bear and
The Athol Highlanders
turning and turning
until those courses merge
and are replaced by
a song still more rampant
and the young lad, now a lad no more
finds himself in the midst of his war

on another world
circling a star in the Belt of Orion
facing the enemy in battle
on Farhaven
at the butcher's place called
Killthunder Station

The neighbors
all along the lane
begin to stir and awaken
hearing the voice of
of Neil MacCrimmon's pipes
and the song of his youth sacrificed
doors and shuttered windows
complain as they are opened
but there is only silence
from the neighbors themselves
who at first lean out only to listen
then
one by one
step out in their slippers
into the lane
drawn from their homes
to crowd about him
steaming and stern-faced
yet not entirely able
to hide all the deeper feelings
welling up inside

And seeing this
Neil eases into another theme
different from the first

altered and warmed by
grace notes and innumerable
embellishments
until the sorrow and rage are replaced
with a sense of yearning

Is that the MacCrimmon boy?
asks a voice
it must be
says another
but he's so young
says a third
then Annie MacGregor
hisses for
them to be silent and to listen

But Neil's song
is already nearing its close
having reached New Alba
on Finalshore
where his enlistment ends
and the name he lost
at Killthunder
is found again
and having both his freedom
and his name restored
he turns his heart
and he turns his eyes
towards
his home and his Sissy
once more
still watching him

from behind the glass

And so he finishes
with a tune of homecoming
of Hogmanay and Auld Lang Syne
of loving and forgiving
of pain and healing
of letting go and embracing
and most of all
remembering
and hearing this
not even the sun
could hide any longer
breaking through the cold clouds
to shimmer upon the sea of
upturned faces
who smile in the sudden warmth
and with that
all the old colors of the old town
return
yellow
green
red
and blue
all as bright as summer
and new
and this is how
a dark-haired and impossibly
young man
First Foots his entire village
and shares his baby sister's
long promised blessing

giving everything

he has and is

on this

his sisters

final

New Year's morn.

Alas...

I am so ready
to leave this country
everyday
it feels less and less
like home
everyday
it is more threatening
in every possible way
and everyday
I see more and more
incidents of insanity
brutality
outright fuckery
calculated indifference
butchery
and so
much
pain
My wife
who I love more than life
itself
does not feel safe here
anymore
indeed
she is not safe here
and my own heart
is breaking here
so that now at last I think
we must shake the dust
of this country from our souls
and from our boot heels and

together walk away
from Babylon the Great
return to the wilderness
to innocence
and to goodness
before it is to late.

Mieru

Children
first recognize magic
when they look into
a dog's eyes and the dog
looks back into theirs
there is a connection
it is obvious and it is true
bringing smiles
and binging joy
adults mostly
forget this over time
but dogs do not
they remember that moment
yearning ever after
for the child
now grown older
taller and distant
to see again
to recall
to find
the unspoken word
and to know.

Last Night

I dreamed of her funeral
funeral dreams
are difficult dreams
not exactly nightmares
but difficult to cypher
and puzzle out
especially
when the person
lying in the box
stirs
awakens
and sits up
confused
and asking you
what's happening?
to which
you hear yourself
answer saying
you're dead
which is a horrible thing
to say
a horrible thing to hear
I mean
who wants to be told that?
and who wants to be the one
to say that?
who wants to be that?
wouldn't a hug be better?
but funeral dreams
are not a comfort
they feel like omens

so full of dark gravity
filling you with a kind of
singularity
pulling at you
irresistibly
and who wants that sort
of omen waking you up
leaving sitting there
in the dark
confused and
questioning
no one
that's who
absolutely no one
funeral dreams
are difficult dreams
and inevitably
come true.

My Blue Boat

Dig out all the change
from behind the sofa's cushions
and from under the car's seats

Use it to buy that old blue boat
with the peeling paint
and the rotting bottom

Wrap my body in some towels or blankets
and lay me inside
with your sweater under my head as a pillow

Put a picture of the dog in a frame
at my feet
along with a lantern for the light

Then give me to the tide and walk away
don't look back
not even a glance — not even one

Go instead to your favorite shop
take all the time you want — do not hurry
and buy something for yourself that's pretty

That more than anything you could imagine
would make me happy
in the end.

Keys

When I was a very
small boy
five or six or seven
I spent my summer
collecting lost keys
brass keys
steel keys
some shiny
and some tarnished
some all crusty
and green even
house keys
padlock keys
car keys
and keys of total
mystery
I kept them in a jar
by my bed
and sometimes
tried them out
but never once
did I find their locks
yet still they make
me dream.

In Sheep's Clothing

my fears
are now made real
everyday
by imbeciles
and stable geniuses
false prophets and false profits
cooked books
bent laws
judges who bear false witness
cults
brutes
fanatics
cunning men
and those that follow
cunning men
but in my green eyes
behind these
progressive spectacles
that let me see
up close
near
and distant
and with my uncompromised
wits'
and heart that beats
out its own particular rhythm
I know the difference
between a parade
a funeral
and the death march
and I know a good shepherd

from a wolf who grins
above his kill.

Feeling the Apocalypse

I feel a sense of deep foreboding
a tension in the air
of stilled music and coming thunder
that makes me hold my breath and pray
hoping
yet doubtful
that we might yet see
the sunsets of maybe one
or two or three more days
before the seals break
the trumpets sound
and drum-heads pound that
awful march to war
where I am left to play
the role of the witness
and nothing more
helpless
struck dumb and sick
as the false church
with its self-righteous and
misguided rage
manipulates butchers and mutilates
the holy word
and tries to claim my faith as its own
stealing my God's name from my lips
stealing His name from my heart
and rendering the holy spirit
a picture on a flag — a taxidermied bird
a symbol to use and abuse
and nothing more
replacing His voice with the lies

of false prophets, charlatans and hucksters
ministers of deceit and death
who celebrate their anointed leaders
as patriotic saints
anointed only with the cunning lies
and bigotry of a failing race
that chooses hate over love
and vainglorious victories
over surrender and grace
Paradise is lost now
again
and I hear the locusts stirring underground
answering Abaddon's call
beating their new wings
aching to be born
and my neck tingles for it — tingles where
the blade will fall
and so I feel it now so clearly
that sense of deep foreboding
a tension in the air
of stilled music and coming
thunder
and the apocalypse unfolding.

Rivers

Rivers
so easy to recall
easy even to imagine
wide
slow
deep
peaceful
shallow
swift
violent
loud
there is no water
as refreshing
as the river's water
especially in the spring
flowing down from
the high country
and the thaw
of melting snow
singing almost
as it flows over steep
stones and wide
slabs of granite talus
rivulets of the purest water
joining brooks
and becoming streams
all life is fed by rivers
and the rivers themselves
are life
but
it is easy to forget

easy to let the stream of time
wash the memory away
and take the knowledge
and the feelings
of the water upon our flesh
of the water flowing about us
and of the water carrying us
it is easy to forget what it is
to be alive
but the river remains
it is still there
one of many
and all of one
when I return to the river
at the end of my life
I will let it take me again
I will weep with joy
and rejoice in my
tears.

Shiny

You
are as beautiful as
that shiny silver dollar
I once found
at the blue bottom
of the swimming pool
when I was nine
liberty's face in profile
and my eyes blinded
by all that wet sunlight
that I suddenly held in the
palm of my hand
magical and
making my heart
flutter
as with a dozen
feathered wings
set loose
inside my chest.

30

In the end
when everything
has been said
that must be said
and everything
has been done
that might be done
we will pause
remove our hats
wipe the sweat
from our brow and
from our neck
and we will rest
taking our last breath
too soon
we will forget
and so we will be
forgotten
erased by indifferent
nature
by the rain and the wind
or by envious men
with their own cruel
and cunning goals
or by the very hand
of God almighty
who knows
what good may come
of a man
and what good in the end
a man has left undone.

ACKNOWLEDGEMENTS:

In closing, I would like to offer a special thank you to my good friend Earl
T. Roske, who first suggested this project and then took on the greater task
of editing and producing the actual book. I wrote these poems, but it was
Earl who did the heavy lifting that brought this book to life.
Thank you for your friendship, support and patience.

Andrew